The
Monster Problem

A Red Fox Book
Published by Random House Children's Books
20 Vauxhall Bridge Road, London SW1V 2SA
A division of The Random House Group Ltd
London Melbourne Sydney Auckland
Johannesburg and agencies throughout the world

1 3 5 7 9 10 8 6 4 2

First published in Great Britain by Hutchinson Children's Books 1989
Red Fox edition 1991
This edition 2000

Printed in Singapore by Tien Wah Press (PTE) Ltd

THE RANDOM HOUSE GROUP Ltd Reg. No. 954009
www.randomhouse.co.uk

The MONSTER Problem

INGRID AND DIETER SCHUBERT

'I'm brave,' cried Peggy one morning, 'as brave as a lion and as fierce as a tiger.' And she roared and growled, ready for any adventure.

When she opened her curtains, there was the adventure waiting for
her in the garden. Four huge legs and four great arms were
appearing through the mist.

In a second Peggy was up and dressed.

Mum and Dad were fast asleep. 'Grrrrrr!' cried Peggy in her loudest voice. 'There's a monster in our garden. He's bigger than our house, bigger than our trees!'

'How nice,' said Mum, who rolled over and went straight back to sleep.

Peggy put on her shoes and ran outside.

'*There* you are,' boomed a deep voice. 'I've been waiting for you all night long.'

'For me, why?' asked Peggy.

'Because we've got a monster of a problem and we need someone as brave as a lion and as fierce as a tiger to help us.'

'That's me,' replied Peggy. 'I'll come, but I'd better tell Mum first.'

'You again,' sighed Mum, wearily.

'The monster wants me to fly away with him,' said Peggy. 'He has a problem and he needs my help.'

'Well, make sure you're back for breakfast,' said Mum.

Peggy climbed aboard. 'Hold tight,' cried the monster, who was called Mumbly.
   He ran like the wind.

In no time at all they were high above the houses.

'Wheeeeeee!' cried Peggy.

They flew for miles and miles; out of the city, over the villages and through a deep, dark forest where Mumbly landed in a clearing. Bump!

Peggy saw two more monsters emerge from the trees.

'Here are Rumbly and Grumbly,' said Mumbly.

'Is this all you could find,' grumbled Grumbly.

'But she's as brave as a lion and as fierce as a tiger,' replied Mumbly. 'Her name is Peggy, and she's come to solve our problem.'

The monsters smiled. 'Well, Peggy-brave-as-a-lion, we'd better tell you what it is.'

Rumbly began. 'We are strawberry-eating monsters,' he explained. 'And once upon a time we lived very happily, playing hide-and-seek by day and feasting on strawberries by night. They grew in their hundreds hereabouts and there was enough for everybody.'

'Then one night,' continued Mumbly, 'I heard a rustling, crackling noise. And when I opened one eye a terrifying voice hissed:

"Keep your eyes shut or sorry you'll be.
I'm taking these strawberries home for my tea!"

And in the morning our whole supply of strawberries was gone.'

'A strawberry thief!' said Peggy. 'I will catch him.'
  'Catch him?' cried Mumbly. 'But he's a dangerous wild animal.'
  'Not to someone who's as brave as a lion and as fierce as a tiger.
Grrrrrrr!' cried Peggy.

'Now let's get to work. We must pick as many strawberries as we can and make a pile,' she said. When they had finished the three monsters hid behind Peggy and waited.

Very soon there was a rustling noise. 'It's him,' whispered Rumbly.
The three monsters closed their eyes, but Peggy watched as the
strawberry pile began to move. Silently, she crept around the tree.
The huge shadow of the strawberry thief loomed up.
    'Grrrrrrrrrrr!' cried Peggy, as brave as a lion and as fierce as
a tiger.

'Gotcha!'

One by one, Rumbly, Mumbly and Grumbly emerged from the trees. The thief was a small, fat squashy monster with a strawberry nose.

'Why, it's nothing but a splodge-nose,' said Grumbly in disbelief.
'Fancy us being afraid of *that*!'

The splodge-nose explained. 'I am sorry,' he said, 'but I too love
strawberries, and they do not grow where I live.' He sounded so sad
that Rumbly, Mumbly and Grumbly decided to be kind.

'You can stay with us,' said Grumbly. 'But you must replace all the strawberries you have stolen. We will help.'

They worked very hard and soon there was enough to last the whole summer, and longer. The store was complete and they were ready for a game of hide-and-seek.

Peggy found all the monsters, except for one.

She knew where to find him.

Sure enough, there he was in the place where the strawberry pile had been. Now there were none left!

'Grrrrrrr,' said Peggy, crossly. 'It seems I haven't solved the problem after all.' Then she looked at her watch. 'Quick, it's breakfast time, I must get back.' Before he had time to think, Peggy grabbed the splodge-nose and climbed on to Mumbly's back.

'I'm taking the problem with me,' she cried, as she waved goodbye to Grumbly and Rumbly. 'And you'd better behave,' she added sternly to the splodge-nose.

'Goodbye, and thank you Mumbly,' said Peggy when they arrived
home. 'We're back, Mum,' she cried, 'and I've invited a little
monster for breakfast. I hope you don't mind.'

'That's nice dear,' said Mum. 'Now sit down at the table, it's your
favourite today — toast and *strawberry* jam!'